Melissa's Octopus and other Unsuitable Pets

CHARLOTTE VOAKE

WALKER BOOKS
AND SUBSIDIARIES
LONDON · BOSTON · SYDNEY · AUCKLAND

Here is Melissa's octopus.

What a splendid creature he is.

Unfortunately, an octopus is not a very suitable pet.

You should see the mess he makes in the bathroom!

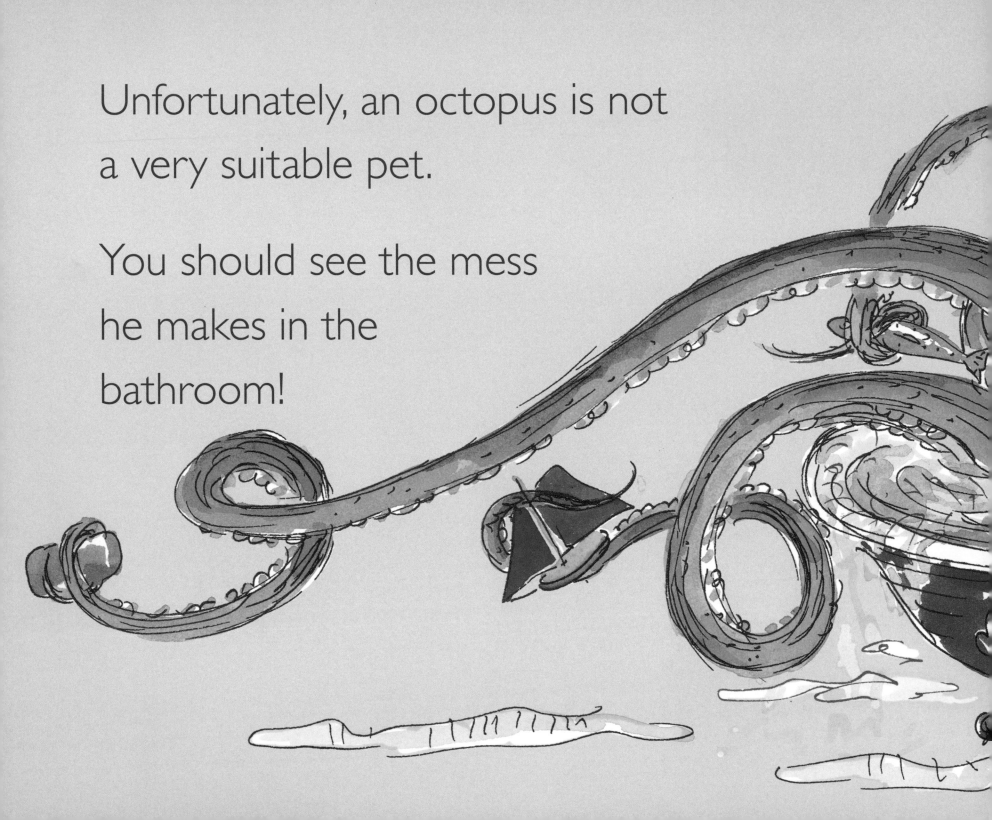

Thomas has a much
smaller pet –
a lovely little mole.
But the mole is always
digging tunnels,
which makes him
very hard to find.

Thomas never knows
where he'll pop up next.

Poor Betty!

She can never find her pet either.

He's a chameleon.

Where can he be today?

This is Arthur's warthog.

Isn't he a beautiful animal!

But a warthog is not a great pet.
A warthog does exactly what it wants.

Caroline's giraffe is a gentle pet
with lovely long legs.

But she's a bit too tall for Caroline.

This is Simon's worm.

He's not a bad pet, but Simon never knows which end to talk to.

This is Peter's elephant.
He is very big.

He is also VERY heavy.

Sometimes he's upstairs…

and he ends up
downstairs by
mistake.

Kevin and Bertrand
are very proud of their new pet crocodile.
They have invited Melissa, Thomas, Betty, Arthur,
Caroline, Simon and Peter round to see it.

Look at its glittering teeth!

And where
are Melissa, Thomas,
Betty, Arthur, Caroline,
Simon and Peter?

Phew!

They're all having
tea together.

But next time they'd
better watch out…

A crocodile really is …

the MOST UNSUITABLE PET OF ALL!

To my
beautiful
badly ~ behaved
pet parrot
Gwen

First published 2014 by Walker Books Ltd 87 Vauxhall Walk, London SE11 5HJ • 2 4 6 8 10 9 7 5 3 1 • © 2014 Charlotte Voake
The right of Charlotte Voake to be identified as author/illustrator of this work has been asserted by her in accordance
with the Copyright, Designs and Patents Act 1988 • This book has been typeset in Gill Sans Light • Printed in China • All rights
reserved. No part of this book may be reproduced, transmitted or stored in an information retrieval system in any form
or by any means, graphic, electronic or mechanical, including photocopying, taping and recording, without prior written
permission from the publisher. • British Library Cataloguing in Publication Data: a catalogue record for this book is
available from the British Library • ISBN 978-1-4063-5300-6 • www.walker.co.uk